DINO-HALLOWEEN

LISA WHEELER

ILLUSTRATIONS BY BARRY GOTT

CAROLRHODA BOOKS · MINNEAPOLIS

Text copyright © 2019 by Lisa Wheeler
Illustrations copyright © 2019 by Barry Gott

Carolrhoda Books®
An imprint of Lerner Publishing Group, Inc.
241 First Avenue North
Minneapolis, MN 55401 USA

For reading levels and more information, look up this title at www.lernerbooks.com.

Main body text set in Churchward Samoa 22/36. Typeface provided by Chank.
The illustrations in this book were created in Adobe Illustrator, Photoshop, and Corel Painter.

Library of Congress Cataloging-in-Publication Data

Names: Wheeler, Lisa, 1963– author. | Gott, Barry, illustrator.
Title: Dino-Halloween / Lisa Wheeler ; Illustrated by Barry Gott.
Description: Minneapolis : Carolrhoda Books, [2019] | Summary: The dinosaurs enjoy a variety of Halloween activities, including visiting a haunted house, carving pumpkins, and trick-or-treating.
Identifiers: LCCN 2018041032 (print) | LCCN 2018047924 (ebook) | ISBN 9781541561069 (eb pdf) | ISBN 9781512403176 (lb : alk. paper)
Subjects: | CYAC: Stories in rhyme. | Dinosaurs—Fiction. | Halloween—Fiction.
Classification: LCC PZ8.3.W5668 (ebook) | LCC PZ8.3.W5668 Dhp 2019 (print) | DDC [E]—dc23

LC record available at https://lccn.loc.gov/2018041032

Manufactured in the United States of America
1-39168-21082-1/16/2019

Come October, nights are longer.

Moon looms bigger. Winds blow stronger.

Air is crisper. Leaves are falling.

Dino-Halloween is calling!

Hayrides! Pumpkins! So much fun!
The dinos spot a field and run.

Pick a pumpkin off the vine.
Minmi hollers, "This one's mine!"

Compy's choice is just his size.

"Someone want to help me, guys?"

Fat ones, thin ones, tall or wide—
Apatosaurus can't decide.

Back across the ground they race.
Time to carve a pumpkin face!

Some are cute and some are spooky.
Troodon's looks kind of kooky.

Iguanodon has no finesse.
He's smeared with pumpkin. What a mess!

Grimace, grin, or smiling wide?
Apatosaurus can't decide.

At night, beneath the full moon's shine, nervous dinos stand in line.

They shiver at the shrieks and moans that echo from this haunted home.

Each **Ptero** hangs on to his twin.
Pachy wears an anxious grin.
They all hold hands and . . .
"Step. Right. In."

Ghost and ghoulies! Screams and bumps!
Flashing lights and jittery jumps!

Gruesome clowns and graveyard stones!
Skeletons with clacking bones!

Triceratops is terrified.
T. rex squeals and runs outside.

The others make it to the end.
They know the spooks are just pretend.

Costumes take a lot of thought.
Some want homemade. Some want bought.

Raptor stuffs his clothes with hay—
a scarecrow made the easy way!

Maia makes bright wings herself.
Galli crafts a magic elf.

Tricera is a clown this year.
T. rex wears his hockey gear.

The store explodes with Halloween—
frightful costumes, masks of green.
Pachy tries on wigs and hats.
The **Twins** swoop down as vampire bats.

Diplo likes the black feline.
Allo chooses Frankenstein.

Pirate, penguin, beast, or bride?
Apatosaurus can't decide.

They head down to the Costume Ball.
It's party time for one and all!

Minmi plays the ring-toss game.
Wowza! She has perfect aim!

Apple bobbing makes a splash.
The **Twins** join the three-legged dash.

This party's jumpin'! What a bash!

"Let's get down to the Monster Mash!"

Dancing dinos feel the beat—

move their arms and stomp their feet.

But soon it's time to . . .

TRICK OR TREAT!

Homes are decked for Halloween.
Cobwebs set a spooky scene.

Jack-o'-lanterns stand in rows.
Eyes and grins cast eerie glows.

There's a cauldron! There's a broom!
Look, a witch's potion room!

Dinos run from door to door
for candy, yes, but so much more!

Shiny apples, bags of chips,
popcorn balls, and waxy lips.

The **Ptero Twins** get quite a scare.

"How'd a toothbrush get in there?!"

Bushed from hitting every street,

the dinosaurs want something sweet.

They stop to see **Apatosaur**.

What do they spot inside his door . . . ?

A fretful giant on the floor!

Chocolate bar or popcorn ball?
Apatosaurus wants it all!

Carmel swirls or candy corn?
Apatosaurus feels quite torn.

Tips the bucket. Opens **W-I-D-E.**
Apatosaurus CAN decide!

The dinos walk home with their friends.

They're sleepy as the evening ends.

They drag their bags. They stretch and yawn.

Halloween has come and gone.

They look up to the harvest moon
and hope their tummies still have room . . .

'Cause Dino-Thanksgiving
is coming soon!